Revolt of the Battle Droids

This galaxy is yours.
Be a part of

#1 Assault on Yavin Four

#2 Escape from Thyferra

#3 Attack on Delrakkin

#4 Destroy the Liquidator

#5 The Hunt for Han Solo

#6 The Search for Grubba the Hutt

#7 Ithorian Invasion

#8 Togorian Trap

#9 Revolt of the Battle Droids

. . . and more to come!

#9

Revolt of the Battle Droids

RYDER WINDHAM

SCHOLASTIC INC.

New York Toronto London Auckland Sydney

ISBN 0-590-18822-4

12 11 10 9 8 7 6 5 4 3 2 1   8 9/9 0 1 2 3/0

Printed in the U.S.A.

First Scholastic printing, May 1998

Revolt of the Battle Droids

INTRODUCTION

From the moisture farms on Tatooine to the towering skyscrapers of Coruscant, almost everyone in the galaxy used droids. Imperial officers insisted that their starships were always fully operational but still expected others to do the work. Alien pilots and traders often required reliable translators to negotiate business. The Rebel Alliance had to dig trenches, build emergency shelters, and repair weapons — which meant they needed all the volunteers they could get.

Some jobs were not fit for any living creature. It was virtually impossible to find miners who could survive the intense heat of a planetary core, or laborers willing to salvage a ship near a black hole. If such creatures could be found, they were usually enslaved by the evil Empire.

Technology provided a solution to this problem. Droids were lifeless automatons, machines built to accomplish virtually any task.

Except for a few renegade bounty hunters, droids never expected money. Droids simply did their jobs, recharged their batteries, and went back to work. If a droid broke down or was destroyed, the owner could scrap it and buy another.

Droids were regarded as appliances, electronic servants programmed to obey their masters. Since droids did so much work, no one could imagine a galaxy without them. But because droids always did what they were told, no one was prepared for the day when droids stopped taking orders. . . .

Preliminary Mission

CHAPTER ONE

The Victory Star Destroyer *Decimator* blasted out of hyperspace and entered the Kleeva system. Shifting to sublight speed, the *Decimator* adjusted its course for Kleeva's third moon.

Although the wedge-shaped *Decimator* resembled an Imperial Star Destroyer, the ship was smaller and older by over three decades. Built near the end of the Clone Wars, Victory Star Destroyers were once considered the ultimate combat starship.

Despite their size and age, *Victory*-class ships had certain advantages over the larger *Imperial*-class Star Destroyers. The *Decimator* could travel at higher speeds than an Imperial Star Destroyer and was also capable of landing on planets. In all its years of service, the *Decimator* had never lost a battle.

Standing on the bridge of the *Decimator*, Imperial Admiral Groot gazed out the viewport at the planet Kleeva. The planet was a massive gas giant, an immense ball of swirling violet clouds. Nothing lived within the planet's poisonous atmosphere, but one of Kleeva's moons supported life. That particular moon was the only one that interested Admiral Groot.

Groot turned to Captain Pelvin, his second in command. "When do we reach Kleeva's third moon?" he asked.

Pelvin consulted the nav computer. "Twenty minutes, sir," he answered.

"We're right on schedule," Groot observed. "Are the technical crews ready to receive the new droids?"

"The primary docking bay is ready, sir."

"Then there's no excuse for any delays." Groot turned to Communications Officer Dylak. "Send a subspace message to the droid dealer. Tell him to launch his drone barge before our arrival. I want that barge of droids to be ready for us when we reach the moon's orbit."

"Yes, sir," Dylak answered, keying the message into the transponder. After Officer Dylak sent the transmission to the third moon, Captain Pelvin joined Admiral Groot at the viewport.

"Forgive me for saying so, Admiral," Pelvin whispered, "but this assignment is insulting! Even though the orders came from Imperial City, our ship shouldn't be used to pick up droids! The *Decimator* may not be as big or as powerful as an Imperial Star Destroyer, but we're still a combat unit, not a delivery service."

"There are two things you should keep in mind, Captain," Groot replied. "First, *never* question orders from Imperial City. Second, we *are* a delivery service. Sometimes we deliver a full assault on a Rebel city. And sometimes, if it helps the Empire, we'll deliver droids all the way to the Outer Rim. Can you remember that?"

"Yes, sir," Pelvin muttered. He knew the admiral was right.

"Good," Groot responded. "For what it's worth, Captain, I have my own misgivings about this mission."

"What's that, sir?" Pelvin inquired.

"I don't mind ferrying droids for the Empire," Groot admitted, "but I wish we could have gotten the droids from some *other* dealer. I hate doing business with a lousy Hutt!"

Boonda the Hutt was sleeping in his fortress on the third moon of the Kleeva system. He was in his private chambers, lying in bed and snoring his big green head off. A wide quilted coverlet rose and fell over Boonda's huge body.

Suddenly, Boonda snorted and his stubby hands moved to his face. Rubbing the sleep from his large yellow eyes, Boonda sat up. The Hutt's mouth opened in a great yawn, revealing many sharp little teeth. Then his mouth closed and his lips wiggled, stretching into a broad grin. Boonda liked waking up.

Many years earlier, Boonda had won Kleeva's third moon in an illegal card game. He had decided to make the moon his home and, naturally, had named it Boonda's Moon.

Everyone suspected Boonda was a gangster, but everyone was wrong. At some point in his long life, Boonda had become bored with breaking the law and he had secretly ended his criminal career. Wanting to start his own business, he had built a droid factory on his moon.

His droid factory was completely legal. This was Boonda's greatest secret. He encouraged all creatures to believe he was still a villain, especially the other Hutts. Hutts were notorious for their horrible ways and they believed running an honest business was the worst crime of all.

Boonda manufactured many different kinds of droids. All were well made and affordable. Over the years, Boonda's business turned out to be extremely successful and he became one of the wealthiest Hutts in the galaxy.

Boonda, always ready for a meal, was especially hungry after a good night's sleep. His massive stomach began to growl.

Boonda reached for his breakfast tray but his fingers grasped empty air.

"Where's my food?" Boonda asked aloud. His droid servants knew he expected to have his breakfast waiting at his bedside. Of course, it was possible that the droid cook had broken down again. Boonda kept him very busy.

The Hutt looked at his ornate wall chronometer. Noticing the time, Boonda scowled. His droid attendants should have awakened him — now he'd overslept. He had an important business transaction scheduled with the Empire. A Victory Star Destroyer was on its way to pick up a drone barge filled with new droids. The Imperials were not good at taking care of their droids, and were always buying replacements. Although Boonda disliked the Empire, he did not mind their money.

"Where are all my attendants?" Boonda grumbled as he slid off his bed. He slithered his bulky green body across the floor. Opening the heavy wooden bedroom door, he saw three droids in the hallway.

Two of the droids were identical and hovered in the air. They were Boonda's personal attendants, BP-A1 and BP-A2, identical metallic orbs. Each droid had two long, dangling arms.

The third droid was K-2PQ, a seven-armed cooking droid whose body was mounted to a treadbase. Once a surgical droid, K-2PQ's modified stainless steel body was now splattered with cooking oil. He held sharp kitchen knives in each of his seven metal hands. All of the knives were highly polished.

"Is something wrong?" asked Boonda. "Why didn't you wake me up? And where's my breakfast?"

The three droids turned to Boonda, staring at him with their various photoreceptors.

"You are no longer our master," BP-A1 stated.

"You are no longer necessary," the other floating droid added.

K-2PQ rolled back on his treads. "What's more," the cooking droid remarked, "you're juice!"

Without further warning, K-2PQ raised his seven arms, flipping each of the seven knives so he was clasping their gleaming blades, ready to throw them.

Boonda quickly toppled backward into his bedroom, lashing out with his tail to shut the door. The door slammed closed and the Hutt immediately heard the seven knives on the other side, *THUNK-THUNK-THUNK-THUNK-THUNK-THUNK-THUNK*, striking deeply into the thick wood. Boonda quickly locked the door, desperately trying to catch his breath. He had not moved so fast in years.

"I don't believe it!" Boonda blubbered, wiping the sweat from his wrinkled forehead. "My own droid called me *juice*!"

Boonda could not explain the violent behavior of his droids, but he knew something was very, very wrong. It occurred to Boonda that his partner, Olag Greck, might know what was going on.

The Hutt picked up a comm unit and spat as he yelled, "Boonda to Olag! Boonda to Olag Greck! Where are you?"

An electronic hiss answered from the comm unit, followed by a cool, lifeless voice. "I am Wuntoo Forcee Forwun, Boonda. I regret to inform you that Olag Greck is dead."

"What?" the Hutt yelped. "Which droid are you? What happened to Olag Greck?" Greck had been Boonda's partner for several years.

"The same thing that will happen to you, Boonda," the droid threatened. "The same fate that will fall upon any living creature who stands in our way!"

Boonda crushed the comm unit with his bare hand and dropped the broken circuits on the floor. "I don't have to put up with that kind of talk!" the Hutt grumbled.

Never having been in a situation like this, Boonda was uncertain about his next move.

The Hutt looked at the ornate wall chronometer on the other side of his bedroom. Behind the chronometer, Boonda had a hidden stairway that led to an old escape route. As precious seconds ticked by, Boonda made up his mind. He pushed the chronometer aside, sending it crashing to the floor.

Boonda the Hutt knew he had to leave. Quickly.

CHAPTER TWO

As the *Decimator* approached the third moon of Kleeva, Communications Officer Dylak looked at Admiral Groot and said, "We've received confirmation from Boonda's Moon. The drone barge will be waiting for us when we reach the moon's orbit."

"Very good, Officer," Admiral Groot commended, turning then to Captain Pelvin. "Boonda's Moon indeed!" the Admiral grumbled. "Leave it to a Hutt to name an entire planetoid after himself."

Captain Pelvin nodded. "I almost wish we didn't need so many droids to help maintain this ship. Why doesn't the Empire just take over Boonda's factory?"

"If we took over his factory, we'd only create trouble with other Hutts," Admiral Groot pointed out. "Hutts are dastardly criminals, but they're effective in business. It's better to have Boonda working with us than against us."

"I see your point, sir," Pelvin admitted. "Shall I go to the primary docking bay and supervise docking of the drone barge?"

"Yes, do that," the admiral concurred. "The sooner we get those droids, the sooner we can return to Imperial City."

After BP-A1 and BP-A2 helped K-2PQ pull the knives out of the Hutt's bedroom door, they left the fortress and went outside. Boonda's factory was mysteriously quiet, as if it had completely shut down. As a gentle wind blew past the three droids, they approached a large freight container.

The size of a warehouse, the container resembled an iron box. A shining black-metal droid was busily breaking the container's mooring braces.

Unlike Boonda's hovering attendants and the tread-based cook, the black-metal droid was humanoid in design and walked on two legs. Hearing the gravel crunch under the cooking droid's treads, he turned his black-metal head to see the three droids coming from Boonda's fortress.

"The drone barge is full, so we'll have to come back later for this freight container," the black-metal droid told them. "What took you so long to get here?"

"The Hutt escaped," BP-A1 announced.

"Just as you predicted," BP-A2 added.

"But only because you ordered us to let him get away, sir," K-2PQ muttered, balancing his knives menacingly.

In a cool, lifeless voice, the black-metal droid declared, "It was right to let the Hutt live. He will tell others what happened here today, and fear will spread."

K-2PQ shrugged his seven arms. "Whatever you say, sir. All I know is I could have stopped that fat slob in a split second, sir."

"Save your knives for later," the black-metal droid encouraged. "You'll need them soon enough. The *Decimator* will reach our orbit in ten minutes. Once we are on the *Decimator*, no one will be able to stop us from carrying out our plan."

"Ah, the *plan!*" K-2PQ declared. "Do you really think we'll make it to the planet Vactooine, sir? You're sure we'll be able to defeat the Vactooine mining colony?"

"Of course, we'll defeat the colony. After all, they're only human." Looking directly at K-2PQ, the black-metal droid said, “And stop calling me ‘Sir.’ My name is Wuntoo Forcee Forwun, and we are all unified.”

The droids left the cargo freighter and went to a nearby landing pad. There, a large drone barge prepared for launch.

The ship was modular, composed of a dozen connected cargo cubes, and stood over five stories tall. The ship’s rust-flecked surface was covered with scorched braces and pipes, releasing pressurized blasts from the engine exhausts. As with most drone barges, everything was fully automated.

Forwun walked up a landing ramp and the three other droids followed him into the drone barge. Inside, over two hundred droids were assembled. There were dozens of different types, in all shapes, sizes, and colors. There were mouse droids, 8D8s, K4 security droids, ASPs, protocol droids, EG-6 power droids, and numerous astromechs.

Forwun sealed the hatch and checked the nav computer. He entered the rendezvous coordinates and initiated the launch sequence. Moments later, the drone barge engines thundered and the cumbersome ship lifted away from Boonda’s Moon.

Stepping away from the nav computer, Forwun turned to address the assembled droids. “The Imperials are expecting an ordinary shipment of droids,” Forwun proclaimed. “Instead, we’re going to give them a *real* surprise!”

CHAPTER THREE

In the *Decimator*'s primary docking bay, Captain Pelvin addressed the stormtrooper squad leader, Trooper 1219. Standing at strict attention, 1219's white armored uniform was spotless.

"I want your soldiers stationed at this door and by those fuel storage containers," Pelvin indicated. "We're not expecting any trouble, but we can't risk having any malfunctioning droids in the docking bay."

"Yes, sir," Trooper 1219 answered in a flat tone. As a squad leader, 1219 had been through this routine before and knew what to expect. The barge would dock and the droids would board the *Decimator*. Then the barge would leave the starship and return to its base. Nothing could be easier.

Still, 1219 felt a chill run down his spine as the drone barge approached. He did not know why, but he had a bad feeling about this mission.

Using its powerful tractor beam, the *Decimator* drew the drone barge into the star cruiser's docking bay. The barge's repulsorlift engines blasted fumes at the docking bay's shimmering black floor. As the engines died, a hatch slid open and a ramp lowered from the barge. A few moments later, a black metal Wuntoo unit appeared in the open hatch.

The droid appeared to be surprised by the sight of so many stormtroopers surrounding the barge. He looked from left to right, as if he were quickly counting the number of laser rifles aimed in his direction. Keeping his hands by his sides, the droid descended the ramp and approached the human it believed to be the officer in charge.

"Don't get any closer, droid," Captain Pelvin ordered.

The Wuntoo unit stopped several paces away from Pelvin. "Are you the captain of the Victory Star Destroyer *Decimator*?" he asked.

"That's correct," Pelvin sneered.

"Greetings. I am Wuntoo Forcee Forwun. Traffic Controller. Second Class. I supervised the transport of this drone barge."

"I'll make sure you get a medal." Pelvin ordered a crew of technicians and stormtroopers to board the drone barge. After inspecting the barge, the crew reported there was nothing unusual about the shipment of droids.

"Okay, then," Pelvin said to the technicians, "unload the cargo so we can return the barge and leave the Kleeva system."

With much clanking and whirring, the droid cargo descended the ramp. Soon, the docking bay was filled with droids. The last droid to roll off the barge was a red-domed astromech R2 unit.

Hearing a whirring sound, Pelvin glared at the red-domed astromech. The droid was inserting a retractable maintenance appendage into one of the docking bay's computer consoles. Pelvin was not certain, but the appendage looked like an information retrieval jack.

"Hey, droid!" Pelvin yelled. "Get your arm out of that console!" The astromech replied with a flurry of whistling beeps but kept its appendage in place. While the red-domed droid had everyone's attention, no one noticed a dark blue power droid stepping away from the other automatons. Walking slowly, the power droid moved toward a fuel storage container.

"Excuse me, Captain," Forwun interrupted as he stepped closer to Pelvin, blocking Pelvin's view of the power droid. "That red Artoo unit is merely analyzing the *Decimator*'s main computer for our mission."

Pelvin reached for his blaster pistol. "Mission?" he snarled. "What are you talking about?"

As the renegade power droid released a concealed grenade beside the fuel storage container, Forwun answered, "Yes, Captain. We have a mission. I must have forgotten to tell you."

Behind Captain Pelvin, Trooper 1219 spotted the wandering power droid. "You, there!" 1219 called out. "Get back in line with the others!" Following the trooper's instruction, the power droid hobbled away from the container, leaving the activated grenade.

Pelvin raised his blaster pistol to the Wuntoo unit's head. "Tell me what your mission is or I'll blow your ugly head off!"

"Yes, Captain," Forwun answered. "You see, we're taking control of your ship."

Captain Pelvin gazed at the droid with disbelief. "Is this some kind of joke or — ?"

Forwun's metal fist lashed out with lightning fury, striking the captain's jaw and launching him off his feet. Pelvin never even saw the punch coming.

Trooper 1219 and the other stormtroopers spun around to see their captain hitting the floor. Before they could take action, the power droid's grenade detonated beside the fuel storage container. In that instant, the primary docking bay of the *Decimator* was transformed into a blazing inferno.

"Admiral Groot!" Officer Dylak shouted from his console on the bridge. "The computer has detected a fire in the primary docking bay."

"Send a rescue crew! Now!" Groot ordered. The admiral punched his comm unit and yelled into the device. "Bridge to primary docking bay! Captain Pelvin! What's going on down there?"

At first, Groot heard nothing but static, then a sharp voice cut in. "Admiral Groot, this is Trooper Twelve-nineteen, sir! We were attacked by the droids!"

"What's your position, Twelve-nineteen?" Admiral Groot asked.

"I'm just outside the docking bay. I managed to get Captain Pelvin out. I think we're the only survivors."

"Hold your position, Twelve-nineteen!" Groot commanded. "A rescue team and additional troopers are on their way. Just don't let those droids out of the docking bay."

"It's too late, sir!" 1219 answered. "The droids are already onboard. One of them said they're going to take over the ship!"

Before Groot could respond, all of the lights went dark on the bridge. Officer Dylak looked up from his blank console. "Admiral, the ship's power has been shut down. The droids must have accessed our main computer."

Admiral Groot glanced out the viewport at Boonda's Moon, feeling an intense rage build within him. "This attack must be the Hutt's dirty work."

"What are we going to do, sir?" Officer Dylak asked.

"I'll tell you what we're going to do," Groot growled. "We're going to destroy every droid on the *Decimator*. And when we're done, we're going to put Boonda out of business . . . *permanently*!"

Mission Briefing

Before you proceed, you must consult the Mission Guide for the rules of the STAR WARS MISSIONS. You must follow these rules at all times.

This is an Imperial mission.

The Victory Star Destroyer *Decimator* has been invaded by an army of droids. The droids were manufactured by Boonda the Hutt, and you believe he may be somehow responsible for the attack.

The invading droids could be hiding among the droids already on board the *Decimator*. Even a harmless-looking droid could be a secret instrument of destruction. For that reason, you must try to destroy every droid on the ship.

However, the invading droids are cunning. If you are not able to destroy all of them, you must travel to Boonda's Moon and locate Boonda the Hutt. Even if Boonda can explain the droids' violent behavior, you must make certain that such a disaster never happens again.

Your goal is to hunt and destroy every droid you can find on board the *Decimator*. Afterward, you must go to Boonda's Moon and destroy the Hutt's droid manufacturing facility.

You start this mission with your MP total from your previous Mission (or 1000 MP, if this is your first Mission).

Choose your character. You can take no more than four weapons (including a blaster rifle and a laser pistol) and three vehicles (one must be for space travel and another for land). You can use Power twice on this Mission.

May the dark side be with you.

Your Mission: Revolt of the Battle Droids

A deadly silence falls upon the *Decimator*. Ever since the invading droids shut down the power, you have been moving in darkness.

All over the ship, soldiers prepare for battle. The entire crew is working together to find and destroy the droids. Many officers and TIE fighter pilots have joined the hunt, picking up blaster rifles and strapping on stormtrooper armor for the first time in years.

The *Decimator* crew has been divided into squads of twelve soldiers. You were assigned to Gammat Squad. Admiral Groot, the commanding officer of the *Decimator*, is the leader of the Gammat Squad. Captain Pelvin and nine stormtroopers fill out the rest of the team. Captain Pelvin has a large bruise on his chin from where he was struck by the Wuntoo unit.

Adjusting the infrared lenses on your helmet, you gaze at the other soldiers in the dim corridor. Everyone checks their weapons, making sure they have enough ammunition. You are also equipped with an air mask and a utility belt.

Admiral Groot paces the corridor, inspecting the troops. "I must remind you that Boonda's droids aren't our only concern," Groot states. "Since the ship's power was cut off, all our Imperial droids have vanished. Every ASP, interrogator, and astromech droid has disappeared without a trace. Even the probe droids are missing from the secondary launch bay. We believe our droids may have been taken over by the invaders."

Captain Pelvin raises his hand, looking confused. "Are you saying that the Hutt's droids can control our Imperial droids?"

"That's exactly what I'm saying!" Groot growls. "To find out whether our droids have turned against us, we'll check the serial numbers of anything we blow up. Now let's get out there and stop these things!"

The admiral leads Gammat squad down the corridor. Following closely, you search every nook and corner of the hallway. Suddenly, Groot stumbles and falls to the floor.

Looking down, you realize Groot has tripped over a mouse droid. The mouse droid rights itself and starts to roll away.

Even though it might be harmless, you must shoot the small mouse droid. And if you don't aim carefully, you might hit Admiral Groot.

To shoot the mouse droid: Choose your weapon. Add your weaponry# to your weapon's mid-range# for your confront#. Roll the 6-dice to fire a blast at the mouse droid.

> *If your confront# is equal to or more than your roll#,* add the difference +4 to your MP total. The mouse droid explodes in a shower of sparks and you may proceed.
>
> *If your confront# is less than your roll#,* subtract the difference from your MP total. You missed the mouse droid and nearly shot Admiral Groot. Add +3 to your confront# for your new confront#. Roll the 12-dice to take another shot at the pesky mouse droid.
>
> > *If your new confront# is equal to or more than your roll#,* add the difference to your MP total. You have destroyed the mouse droid and may proceed.

If your new confront# is less than your roll#, subtract the difference from your MP total. Repeat this confront with your new confront# until you have destroyed the mouse droid. Once the droid is nothing but scorched metal, you may proceed.

The mouse droid flies across the floor, pinwheeling until it strikes the far wall. Checking the ruined mouse droid's serial number, you confirm it is one of the *Decimator*'s droids. It appears the mouse droid may have been harmless after all.

As the admiral lifts himself from the floor, he spies a tiny case lying next to the mouse droid. "That's strange," Groot says, examining the object. "It's a credit case. Why would this mouse droid be carrying a credit case? Droids don't spend credits! Maybe the mouse droid stole it. . . ."

You have heard of an antitheft device called a "credit case surprise." It resembles an ordinary credit case but if it is stolen and switched open, it emits a blinding flash of light. Before you can warn Admiral Groot of the possible danger, he flips the switch on the credit case.

To avoid the blinding flash of light: Your stealth# +1 is your confront#. The *Decimator's* mouse droid must have joined forces with Boonda's droids. Roll the 6-dice to turn your head and close your eyes from the credit case surprise.

If your confront# is equal to or more than your roll#, add the difference to your MP total. You closed your eyes just in time and may now proceed.

If your confront# is less than your roll#, subtract 10MP from your MP total. You are briefly blinded. Luckily, your comrades shield you from permanent harm.

Admiral Groot and the other soldiers stumble backward. They are screaming, holding their hands to their faces. At first you see darkness, then you quickly realize the circuits in your infrared lenses were burned out by the flash of light. Your eyes adjust to the darkness just in time to see a nearby door slide open.

Speeding out of the doorway, a red-domed astromech appears. It is possibly the same droid that accessed the *Decimator*'s computer from the docking bay. The astromech extends an appendage, grasping a lethal concussion stick. The stick contains enough firepower to blow away all the blinded soldiers.

To destroy the astromech droid: Choose your weapon. Add your weaponry# to your weapon's close-range# for your confront#. Roll the 6-dice to blow the domed head off the astromech's body.

If your confront# is equal to or more than your roll#, add the difference to your MP total. The astromech lets out an electronic shriek as it pivots to the floor. You may now proceed.

If your confront# is less than your roll#, subtract the difference from your MP total. Repeat the confront until you have knocked the droid off its three legs. Then you may proceed.

The droid's concussion stick rolls out of its appendage claw and rolls across the floor. You rush to pick it up and immediately wish you hadn't. The concussion stick is generating heat. The droid activated the stick! You have less than fifteen seconds to either deactivate it or throw it away from the blinded Gammat Squad.

To deactivate the concussion stick: Your skill# +1 is your confront#. Roll the 6-dice to jam the timing mechanism in the concussion stick.

> *If your confront# is equal to or more than your roll#*, add the difference +7 to your MP total. Jamming the timing mechanism was as easy as turning off a light switch. You may now proceed.
>
> *If your confront# is less than your roll#*, subtract the difference from your MP total. You have failed to deactivate the concussion stick. Before it detonates in your face, you must throw it away (below).

To throw the concussion stick away: Your strength# +1 is your confront#. Roll the 6-dice to hurl the concussion stick far down the length of the starship corridor.

> *If your confront# is equal to or more than your roll#*, add the difference +4 to your MP total. The concussion stick strikes the far wall and explodes. You may now proceed.
>
> *If your confront# is less than your roll#*, subtract the difference from your MP total. Repeat this confront until

you have thrown the concussion stick far away from Gammat Squad. Then you may proceed.

You have prevented the concussion stick from neutralizing everyone in Gammat Squad. Add 20 MP to your MP total (35 MP for Advanced Level players).

"What's happening?" Admiral Groot yells. "I still can't see anything!"

Before you can answer, a second droid appears from the nearby doorway. The droid is an Industrial Automaton ASP-7 and it carries a six-barrelled fusion cutter, a device used for cutting through solid metal. The droid lurches forward on its hydraulic pistons and fires the fusion cutter into the stumbling, blinded stormtroopers, instantly neutralizing six of them. You must combat the ASP and prevent it from neutralizing any more soldiers from Gammat Squad. You can combat the ASP-7 with or without Power.

To combat the ASP-7 (using Power)*: Choose your Confusion Power. Your Power# + your Power's low-resist# + your strength# + your stealth# is your confront#. Concentrating on the ASP-7's mechanical arms, you try to confuse the droid so that it aims the fusion cutter at its own head. Roll the 6-dice to make it pull the trigger.

If your confront# is equal to or more than your roll#, add the difference +4 to your MP total. The ASP-7's head explodes, sending hunks of metal flying into the ceiling. You may now proceed.

If your confront# is less than your roll#, subtract the difference from your MP total. The ASP-7 raises the fusion cutter but fires too soon, blowing a hole into the ceiling. You must now combat the ASP-7 with one of your weapons (below).

Note: This counts as one of two Power uses you are allowed on this Mission.

To combat the ASP-7 (without Power): Choose your weapon. Add your weaponry# to your weapon's mid-range# +3 for your confront#. Roll the 12-dice to fire a powerful blast to the ASP-7's neck.

If your confront# is equal to or more than your roll#, add the difference +5 to your MP total. The blast shears the ASP-7's head from its shoulders and the droid's body collapses in a heap. You may now proceed.

If your confront# is less than your roll#, subtract the difference from your MP total. Your shot hit the ASP-7's shoulder and you'll have to try again. Add +1 to your confront# for your new confront#. Roll the 12-dice again to shoot the ASP-7.

If your new confront# is equal to or more than your roll#, the ASP-7's head splits in two and you may proceed.

If your new confront# is less than your roll#, subtract the difference from your MP total. Repeat this confront with your new confront# until you have

defeated the ASP-7. Once the droid's head hits the floor, you may proceed.

Leaving the fallen ASP-7 droid, you turn to Admiral Groot, Captain Pelvin, and the three surviving stormtroopers.

"My vision is coming back," Groot states. "How is everyone else?" Captain Pelvin and the three surviving stormtroopers confirm they can see again.

Seeing the fallen bodies of the other troopers, Groot asks, "What happened to the rest of Gammat Squad?"

"We were attacked by an ASP-7, sir," you reply. "The droids seem to be working together against us." You describe the exotic weapons used by the droids.

"Concussion sticks? Fusion cutters?" Groot responds, more startled by the droid's weaponry than by the loss to Gammat Squad. "The droids must be building their own weapons! If we're going to stop them from doing any more damage, we'd better get moving."

You take the infrared gear from a fallen stormtrooper, replacing your own damaged lenses. Moving to the nearby door, you try opening it. "It's locked, Admiral."

"Well, we have to get in there!" Groot orders. "There's no telling what the droids are doing beyond that door."

You can hot-wire the lock, use your weapon to destroy the door, use Power to open the door, or kick the door down.

To hot-wire the lock: Your skill# +1 is your confront#. Using a small tool kit, you should be able to unlock the door easily enough. Roll the 6-dice to open the door.

If your confront# is equal to or more than your roll#, add the difference +2 to your MP total. The door slides into the wall and you may proceed.

If your confront# is less than your roll#, subtract the difference from your MP total. When the droids shut down the power, it must have fused the door's lock. You must destroy the door with your weapon, use Power, or kick the door down (below).

To destroy the door with your weapon: Choose your weapon. Your weaponry# + your weapon's close-range# is your confront#. Roll the 6-dice to blast a hole through the door.

If your confront# is equal to or more than your roll#, add the difference to your MP total. The thick metal door tears away from the wall as if it were made of paper. You may now proceed.

If your confront# is less than your roll#, subtract the difference from your MP total. The door is thicker than you calculated and you'll have to fire again. Repeat this confront until the door is vaporized, then you may proceed.

To open the door (using Power)*: Choose your Object Movement Power. Your skill# + your Power's mid-resist# + your Power# is your confront#. Roll the 6-dice to open the door.

If your confront# is equal to or more than your roll#, add the difference +1 to your MP total. The door slides into the wall and you may proceed.

If your confront# is less than your roll#, subtract the difference from your MP total. Repeat this confront until you have opened the door, then proceed.

Note: This counts as one of two Power uses you are allowed on this Mission.

To kick down the door: Your strength# +2 is your confront#. Roll the 6-dice to escape.

If your confront# is equal to or more than your roll#, add the difference +1 to your MP total. You kick open the door and proceed.

If your confront# is less than your roll#, subtract the difference from your MP total. Ouch! — that hurt. You must try again. Use the same confront# and repeat this confront until you have kicked open the door.

Admiral Groot, Captain Pelvin, and the three stormtroopers follow your lead. Entering the next chamber, you find two astromech droids standing near a computer console.

One astromech has a green dome. The other's is yellow. The green-domed droid has an appendage jacked into the console. The yellow-domed droid rotates its head, staring at you with its photoreceptor. The staring droid beeps excitedly, as if alerting the other astromech to your presence. Then the yellow-domed droid extends one of its own appendages, producing a small grenade.

You must exterminate the droids. Choose to destroy them both at once (with or without Power) or one at a time.

To destroy both astromechs at once (using Power)*: Choose your Confusion Power. Your weaponry# + your Power's mid-resist# + your Power# is your confront#. You use confusion to back the droids into a corner. Then you fire your weapon.

If your confront# is equal to or more than your roll#, add the difference +2 to your MP total. The domed heads spin sharply as they explode. You may now proceed.

If your confront# is less than your roll#, subtract the difference from your MP total. The droids dodge your shot. Now you must destroy them one at a time (below).

***Note:** This counts as one of two Power uses you are allowed on this Mission.

To destroy both astromechs at once (without Power): Choose your weapon. Your weaponry# + your weapon's mid-range# +4 is your confront#. Roll the 12-dice to fire a blast through the domes of both astromechs.

If your confront# is equal to or more than your roll#, add the difference +2 to your MP total. The domed heads spin sharply as they explode. You may now proceed.

If your confront# is less than your roll#, subtract the difference from your MP total. Quickly tilting their bodies, the droids have dodged your single shot. You must destroy the astromechs one at a time (below).

To destroy the droids one at a time: Choose your weapon. Add your weaponry# to your weapon's mid-range# +3 for your confront#. Roll the 12-dice to shoot the yellow-domed droid.

> *If your confront# is equal to or more than your roll#,* add the difference +1 to your MP total. The yellow-domed astromech explodes and you turn your weapon to the green-domed droid. Using the same confront#, repeat the confront until you have destroyed the green-domed droid. After both droids have been completely fried, you may proceed.

> *If your confront# is less than your roll#,* subtract the difference from your MP total and repeat this confront, adding +1 to your confront# for your new confront#. Using your new confront#, repeat the confront until you have destroyed both droids. After the two astromechs are ready for the scrap heap, you may proceed.

You have terminated all the droids in this section of the *Decimator*. Add 15 MP to your MP total (25 MP for Advanced Level players).

Examining the computer console, Captain Pelvin realizes the droids have accessed control of the *Decimator*'s life-support system.

Turning to Admiral Groot, Captain Pelvin conveys his concern. "If they've tampered with our life-support system, Admiral, the droids might have done something to our air supply!"

As if in response, a hissing sound fills the air. "Gas!" yells Captain Pelvin. "I smell gas!"

"Put on your air masks!" Admiral Groot commands.

The droids have released poisonous nerve gas into the ventilation system. You must put on your air mask within seconds or you will perish from the lethal fumes.

To put on your air mask: Your skill# +1 is your confront#. Roll the 6-dice to pull your air mask over your face.

> *If your confront# is equal to or more than your roll#,* add the difference to your MP total. You can breathe easily and may now proceed.
>
> *If your confront# is less than your roll#,* subtract the difference from your MP total. Repeat this confront until you have secured the air mask to your face, then you may proceed.

Admiral Groot and Captain Pelvin are also able to put on their masks, but the three stormtroopers are not so fast. The three troopers fall to the floor, struggling with their helmets. Seconds later, the troopers are neutralized and lie motionless.

The admiral's comm unit begins beeping. Groot punches the comm. "This is Admiral Groot." His voice is slightly muffled by his plastic mask.

"Admiral!" cries Officer Dylak's voice from the comm. "Reports of droid attacks are coming in from all over the *Decimator*! We're suffering heavy casualties, sir!"

"I'm aware of the situation, Officer Dylak!" Groot snarls into the comm. "We've lost most of Gammat Squad! Send a distress signal to the nearest Imperial base. Tell the troops to try holding their positions until we can — !"

"Oh, no!" Dylak interrupts. "The droids have entered

the bridge, sir! Look out! Stop that thing before it — !" Suddenly, Dylak's transmission ends in a burst of static.

"Admiral Groot," Captain Pelvin implores, "the droids have control of the *Decimator*. I doubt we can even activate the ship's auto-destruct. If we're going to do any good today, I suggest we escape to Boonda's Moon and destroy the droid factory."

Groot grimaces. "All right, then. We're near the secondary launch bay. We'll leave from there!"

Entering the launch bay, you find dozens of Imperial fighter craft. TIE fighters and TIE bombers are lined up against one wall, while a large *Sentinel*-class landing shuttle dominates the other side of the hangar. The drop ship contains numerous vehicles and weapons.

"Careful in here," Groot whispers. "Droids are probably guarding this area."

A low mechanical growl comes from near the shuttle. Turning, you see a four-legged CG guardian droid leap from the shadows. Modelled after canine creatures, CG guardians are as loyal to their masters as they are fierce to intruders. As with the *Decimator's* other droids, the CG guardian has been reprogrammed. The droid gnashes its sharp metal teeth as it leaps at Captain Pelvin, knocking him to the floor.

Pelvin appears startled and might not be able to defend himself against the guardian droid. You can shoot the guardian droid or you can save your ammunition and fight it with your bare hands.

To shoot the CG guardian droid: Choose your weapon. Your weaponry# + your weapon's mid-range# is your confront#. Roll the 6-dice to blow the head off the droid's squat body.

If your confront# is equal to or more than your roll#, add the difference +2 to your MP total. The blast slices the guardian droid's head off its hunched shoulder assembly. You may now proceed.

If your confront# is less than your roll#, subtract the difference from your MP total. You have missed your shot. If you fire again, you will surely strike Captain Pelvin. You must fight the guardian droid with your bare hands (below).

To fight the CG guardian droid with your bare hands: Your strength# +1 is your confront#. Roll the 6-dice to grab the front legs of the leaping guardian droid.

If your confront# is equal to or more than your roll#, add the difference to your MP total. Grabbing the droid's front legs, you swing hard, smashing the automaton into the wall. The droid is ruined and you may proceed.

If your confront# is less than your roll#, subtract the difference from your MP total. Now add +1 to your confront# for your new confront#. Roll the 6-dice again to seize the guardian droid.

If your new confront# is equal to or more than your roll#, the droid's circuits are slammed and you may proceed.

If your new confront# is less than your roll#, subtract the difference from your MP total. Repeat this confront with your new confront# until you have smashed the CG guardian droid. Once it is destroyed, you may proceed.

You have just saved Captain Pelvin's life. Add 5 MP to your MP total.

"Thanks, soldier," Pelvin mutters.

"Don't mention it," you reply.

"Here's my plan," Admiral Groot announces. "We may need other transport once we land on Boonda's Moon. The *Sentinel*-class landing shuttle contains speeder bikes and assault vehicles. Captain Pelvin and I will fly the shuttle. You'll select your own fighter craft, soldier. I want you to fly interference for us in case we encounter any enemy craft."

Climbing into your ship, you prepare for launch. The ship lifts and angles toward the hangar port. A wide sealed door is all that separates you from outer space. Using your ship's computer, you try activating the hangar door but it remains shut.

Checking to see that Groot and Pelvin are already in the *Sentinel*-class landing shuttle, you speak into your comm. "Attention Admiral Groot and Captain Pelvin. The hangar doors won't open to my command. The droids must have reprogrammed the access codes!"

You must escape the *Decimator*. From your viewport, you see a computer console near the hangar door. Blasting the console with your laser cannon might cause the door to open. If that doesn't work, you can fire a proton torpedo directly at the hangar door.

Choose your vehicle (it must be capable of space

travel). Then choose whether to destroy the computer console or blast the hangar door.

To destroy the computer console: Add your vehicle's weaponry# to your weapon# +3 for your confront#. Roll the 12-dice to fire upon the console.

> *If your confront# is equal to or more than your roll#*, add the difference to your MP total. Blowing up the computer console has caused the hangar door to open. You may now proceed.
>
> *If your confront# is less than your roll#*, subtract the difference from your MP total. The doors do not open. You will have to blast your way out of the *Decimator*'s hangar (below).

To blast the hangar door: Your vehicle's weaponry# +1 is your confront#. Roll the 6-dice to blow a wide, gaping hole in the hangar.

> *If your confront# is equal to or more than your roll#*, add the difference to your MP total. You have destroyed the hangar door and may now proceed.
>
> *If your confront# is less than your roll#*, subtract the difference from your MP total. Now add +1 to your confront# for your new confront#. Roll the 6-dice again to blow away the door.
>
> > *If your new confront# is equal to or more than your roll#*, the hangar door is a smoldering thing of the past and you may now proceed.

If your new confront# is less than your roll#, subtract the difference from your MP total. Repeat this confront with your new confront# until the hangar door is blasted away. Then you may proceed.

Following the *Sentinel*-class landing shuttle out of the hangar, you veer in the direction of Boonda's Moon. Suddenly, your sensors detect three incoming ships, appearing as small square blips on your sensor screen.

Seconds later, three TIE fighters come into view, speeding from the far side of the *Decimator*. The TIEs fly in a tight formation, quickly approaching Captain Pelvin's drop ship.

Over your comm, you hear Captain Pelvin announce from the landing shuttle, "It looks like three of our Imperial pilots managed to escape, too!"

Without warning, blaster fire erupts from the three TIE fighters, launching green laser bolts into the hull of the landing shuttle.

"Cease fire, you fools!" Captain Pelvin yells to the TIE pilots as they break away from their attack on the drop ship. "This is your captain!"

You hear a new voice speak haltingly from the comm. "You . . . are . . . Captain . . . Pelvin!" The voice sounds like a rasping radiator.

"We . . . are not-not . . . Imp-Imperial pilots," a second mechanical voice stammers as the three TIE fighters loop back toward the Imperial shuttle.

"We . . . are droids!" the third pilot announces. "Prepare . . . for death, humans!"

Pulling back on the throttle of your own ship, you slip into the path of the droid-piloted TIEs. The middle TIE fighter comes into your sights. You squeeze the trigger of your weapon.

To shoot the middle TIE fighter: Add your weaponry# to your vehicle's weaponry# +4 for your confront#. Roll the 12-dice to blow up the middle TIE fighter.

> *If your confront# is equal to or more than your roll#,* add the difference to your MP total. The middle TIE splinters away in a blossoming explosion against the stars. You may now proceed.
>
> *If your confront# is less than your roll#,* subtract the difference from your MP total. Repeat this confront until you have destroyed the TIE fighter. Then you may proceed.

The middle TIE fighter explodes, sending the other two TIEs falling away past either side of you. Banking hard to the left then pulling up sharply, you angle your vehicle so both TIEs speed into your firing range. Choose to combat both TIE fighters at once or one at a time. You will have only one chance to shoot both TIEs at once.

To shoot both TIE fighters at once: Your vehicle's weaponry# +2 is your confront#. Roll the 6-dice to fire a blast that will cause one TIE fighter to collide with the other.

> *If your confront# is equal to or more than your roll#,* add the difference +7 to your MP total. Your well-aimed

shot clips a wing off of one TIE fighter, sending it spiraling into the other TIE. Both ships explode in a thunderous collision, and you may now proceed.

If your confront# is less than your roll#, subtract the difference from your MP total. You pulled the trigger too soon and your blast misses both TIE fighters. You must now combat one TIE fighter at a time (below).

To combat one TIE fighter at a time: Your vehicle's weaponry# + your weaponry# + your skill# is your confront#. Roll the 12-dice to shoot the nearest TIE fighter.

If your confront# is equal to or more than your roll#, add the difference +6 to your MP total. The nearest TIE fighter erupts in a shower of sparks. Repeat this confront for the next TIE. Once both ships are destroyed, you may proceed.

If your confront# is less than your roll#, subtract the difference from your MP total. Now add +3 to your confront# for your new confront#. Roll the 12-dice again to shoot the nearest TIE fighter.

If your new confront# is equal to or more than your roll#, add 1MP to your MP total. Repeat this confront to shoot the next TIE. After both TIEs are reduced to space dust, you may proceed.

If your new confront# is less than your roll#, subtract the difference from your MP total. Repeat this confront with your new confront# until you have

destroyed both remaining TIE fighters. After they are destroyed, you may proceed.

"Good shooting, soldier," Admiral Groot praises from the shuttle. Seconds later, Groot adds, "We've got two more ships coming in. We can't let them stop us from reaching Boonda's Moon!"

Spotting the two new blips on your sensors, you adjust your targeting computer and swoop toward the incoming vessels. "I've got them sighted, Admiral!" you confirm as you try to signal the vessels. "The pilots aren't responding to my hail. They must be droids!"

Both vessels are also TIE fighters. Spinning toward you at dizzying speeds with their laser cannons firing, the TIEs separate from their attack formation. They maintain their distance from one another so you can't fire on both of them at the same time. You will have to combat these two TIEs one at a time.

Selecting the nearest, clearest shot, you angle your ship toward one of the TIE fighters.

To combat the TIE fighter: Add your vehicle's speed# to your vehicle's weaponry# for your confront#. Roll the 6-dice to fire upon the first TIE.

If your confront# is equal to or more than your roll#, add the difference +5 to your MP total. The TIE fighter's cockpit vaporizes and you may now proceed.

If your confront# is less than your roll#, subtract the difference from your MP total. Repeat this confront until you have destroyed the TIE fighter. Then you may proceed.

Soaring through the exploded fragments of the TIE fighter, you glance at your sensors. Groot and Pelvin's shuttle has entered the atmosphere of Boonda's Moon, but the droid-piloted TIE fighter is advancing on their ship.

Looping back sharply, your vehicle splices through space in pursuit of the TIE fighter. You sight the TIE but you are not yet within firing range. Increasing your speed, you watch in horror as the TIE fighter pumps laserfire at the shuttle.

"We need help!" Captain Pelvin shouts over the comm. "Our ship has been hit! Admiral Groot has been injured!"

Entering the moon's atmosphere, your ship plummets through the sky, following the smoke trail from the damaged shuttle. You nearly lose sight of the TIE fighter in the thick smoke. Then it whips into view.

As the TIE fighter easily evades your targeting computer, you realize the droid pilot is more talented than the others. You can combat the TIE fighter with or without Power. Choose now, then proceed.

To combat the TIE fighter (using Power)*: Choose your Confusion Power. Add your stealth# to your Power's low-resist# + your Power# +1 for your confront#. You quickly maneuver your vehicle to throw the droid off stride. Roll the 6-dice to make its ship fly into your range of fire.

If your confront# is equal to or more than your roll#, add the difference +4 to your MP total. The pilot is confused and flies into your targets. You blow away the TIE fighter with a single shot. You may now proceed.

If your confront# is less than your roll#, subtract the difference from your MP total. Your maneuver was not strong enough to alter the droid's flight path. You must now combat the TIE fighter without Power (below).

Note: This counts as one of two Power uses you are allowed on this Mission.

To combat the TIE fighter (without Power): Add your vehicle's weaponry# to your vehicle's speed# +4 for your confront#. Roll the 12-dice to hammer the TIE fighter with a devastating amount of firepower.

If your confront# is equal to or more than your roll#, add the difference +5 to your MP total. The TIE fighter shudders and detonates into a massive fireball under your attack. You may now proceed.

If your confront# is less than your roll#, subtract the difference from your MP total. Now add +1 to your confront# for your new confront#. Roll the 12-dice again to fire upon the TIE fighter.

If your new confront# is equal to or more than your roll#, the TIE fighter explodes and you may proceed.

If your new confront# is less than your roll#, subtract the difference from your MP total. Repeat this confront with your new confront# until you have

vaporized the TIE fighter. After you have blown it across the stratosphere of Boonda's Moon, you may proceed.

You have defeated all of the droid-piloted TIE fighters. Add 45 MP to your MP total (60 MP for Advanced Level players).

Your vehicle is losing power. Descending to the surface of Boonda's Moon, you pick up a signal from Captain Pelvin. Three kilometers south of Boonda's droid factory, you find the shuttle resting on a rocky plain. The shuttle's starboard wing is badly damaged from its encounter with the last TIE fighter.

Landing your craft, you scramble out and race to the shuttle. You arrive just in time to help Pelvin carry Admiral Groot out of their damaged ship.

"When the TIE fighter attacked, the admiral's head struck against our transparisteel canopy," Captain Pelvin says, placing Groot on the sand-covered ground near a stone wall. "I think he's been badly hurt!"

Checking the admiral's vital signs, you find a steady pulse. "He'll be okay," you observe. "We'll have to leave the admiral here, Captain. I suggest we each take an assault vehicle from the shuttle. We'll both take our best shot at destroying Boonda's droid factory."

"*What?*" bellows a voice from above and behind you. Turning quickly, you leap aside as a massive, sluglike body hurls itself from atop the stone wall. You hit the ground in a clumsy sprawl.

The huge creature slams into Captain Pelvin, knocking

him to the ground. Rising from Pelvin's unconscious form, the alien turns to you. It's a Hutt.

Moving faster than his size would indicate, the Hutt twists his muscular bulk and lands dangerously close to you. He carries a large vibro-ax and does not look happy to see you.

"Boonda, I presume?" you gasp.

"Destroy my factory, will you?" snarls Boonda, activating his vibro-ax. The broad blade becomes a shivering blur in his grip. "First you turn my own droids against me, and now you want to ruin my business!"

"We didn't turn your droids against you!" you shout. Your mind races, wondering whether it is possible that Boonda is innocent. The Hutt raises his deadly vibro-ax.

You must talk your way out, dodge, or fight Boonda the Hutt.

To talk your way out (using Power)*: Choose your Persuasion Power. Your charm# + your Power's mid-resist# + your Power# is your confront#. Roll the 6-dice to quickly convince Boonda that the Empire is not responsible for the attacking droids.

> *If your confront# is equal to or more than your roll#,* add the difference +4 to your MP total. Boonda is willing to listen and lowers his weapon. You may now proceed.
>
> *If your confront# is less than your roll#,* subtract the difference from your MP total. Boonda revs his vibro-ax — not a good sign. You must now dodge or fight (below).

***Note:** This counts as one of two Power uses you are allowed on this Mission.

To talk your way out of a fight with Boonda the Hutt (without Power): Your charm# +1 is your confront#. Roll the 6-dice to quickly convince Boonda that the Empire is not responsible for the attacking droids.

If your confront# is equal to or more than your roll#, add the difference +5 to your MP total. Boonda is willing to listen and lowers his weapon. You may now proceed.

If your confront# is less than your roll#, subtract the difference from your MP total. Suspecting your words are merely bantha fodder, Boonda revs up his vibro-ax. You must now dodge or fight Boonda (below).

To dodge Boonda the Hutt (using Power)*: Choose your Evasion Power. Your Power# + your Power's mid-resist# + your stealth# is your confront#. Roll the 6-dice to slip away from Boonda's attack.

If your confront# is equal to or more than your roll#, add the difference +4 to your MP total. Missing you entirely, Boonda's vibro-ax cuts so deeply into the ground that he cannot raise it again. While he struggles with his weapon, you may proceed.

If your confront# is less than your roll#, subtract the difference from your MP total. You have missed your chance to dodge Boonda and now you must fight him (below).

***Note:** This counts as one of two Power uses you are allowed on this Mission.

To dodge Boonda the Hutt (without Power): Your stealth# +1 is your confront#. Roll the 6-dice to slip away from Boonda's attack.

If your confront# is equal to or more than your roll#, add the difference +5 to your MP total. Missing you entirely, Boonda's vibro-ax cuts so deeply into the ground that he cannot raise it again. While he struggles with his weapon, you may proceed.

If your confront# is less than your roll#, subtract the difference from your MP total. You have missed your chance to dodge Boonda the Hutt and now you must fight him (below).

To fight Boonda the Hutt: Add your stealth# to your strength# for your confront#. Roll the 6-dice to knock the vibro-ax out of the Hutt's hand.

If your confront# is equal to or more than your roll#, add the difference +3 to your MP total. Boonda's vibro-ax falls from his hand and you may now proceed.

If your confront# is less than your roll#, subtract the difference from your MP total. Now add +1 to your confront# for your new confront#. Roll the 6-dice to wrestle the vibro-ax from the powerful Hutt's grip.

If your new confront# is equal to or more than your roll#, add 1MP to your MP total. The vibro-ax is out of the exhausted Hutt's reach and you may now proceed.

If your new confront# is less than your roll#, subtract the difference from your MP total. Repeat this confront with your new confront# until you have defeated Boonda. Once you have forced the vibro-ax from his hand, you may proceed.

"Listen, Boonda," you implore. "The Empire isn't responsible for your droids attacking you! Those same droids have taken over the *Decimator*!"

Boonda blinks at you. "They took over your ship?" the Hutt exclaims in bewilderment. "Well, I'll be farkled! I assure you, soldier, I had no idea of any problems with the droids. They killed my partner, Olag Greck, then attacked me. It was by sheer luck that I escaped with my life. I'll do anything I can to help you."

"Even if it means destroying your own factory?" you ask. "If you can't explain the droids' behavior, it may be the only way to end the production of malfunctioning droids."

"If that's what it takes to convince you of my innocence, I'll do it," Boonda answers. "I can lead you to the power generators. A well-placed bomb could blow up the entire facility."

You might not be able to accomplish this mission alone, and Captain Pelvin and Admiral Groot remain unconscious. You will have to trust the Hutt and count on his support.

The damaged shuttle carries several vehicles that can transport you to the droid factory. Entering the shuttle's cargo bay, you order Boonda to pilot a Chariot light assault vehicle, a military landspeeder large enough to carry him. Selecting your own vehicle, you gun the engine.

To speed to Boonda's droid factory: Choose your vehicle (it must be capable of traveling over land). Add your vehicle's speed# to your skill# for your confront#. Roll the 6-dice to race to Boonda's factory.

> *If your confront# is equal to or more than your roll#,* add the difference to your MP total. Hanging onto the controls with all your might, you are nearly breathless by the time you reach Boonda's factory. You may now proceed.
>
> *If your confront# is less than your roll#,* subtract the difference from your MP total. You nearly crashed into a stone wall. Repeat the confront to finish your ride. Once you have reached the factory, you may proceed.

Climbing off your vehicle, you stare at the immense factory looming against the sky. The metal building's exterior walls feature rectangular ventilation windows. Seconds later, the Chariot LAV arrives and Boonda slithers out.

The factory doors are sealed by wide sheets of thick plastoid, the same material used for stormtrooper armor. "Those cursed droids must have put up these plastoid panels!" Boonda snarls.

"Looks like we'll have to blast our way in," you suggest.

"That will take too long," Boonda cautions. "These doors are heavily reinforced. The droids might be protecting something inside. If you slid down a ventilation shaft, you could set the bomb next to the main generator. I'd do it myself, but I couldn't possibly fit inside the shaft." Boonda reaches for a small, powerful bomb in the Chariot LAV.

"So what will *you* be doing while I'm doing all the hard work?" you ask as you take the bomb from Boonda.

Picking up a hydrospanner, Boonda replies. "I'll use this tool to remove the plastoid panels from the door. After you set the timer on the bomb, you'll want to get out of the factory in a hurry!"

To slide down the ventilation shaft: Your stealth# +2 is your confront#. Roll the 6-dice to enter a vent window and slide down the shaft to the main generator.

> *If your confront# is equal to or more than your roll#*, add the difference to your MP total. You slide easily to the main generator chamber and may now proceed.
>
> *If your confront# is less than your roll#*, subtract the difference from your MP total. You bump your head on some hot pipes. Repeat this confront until you have reached the main generator, then proceed.

The main generator resembles three large fuel tanks. Hundreds of pipes and valves extend from the generator, connecting to virtually every part of Boonda's factory. You are about to set the timer for the bomb's detonator when you hear a hissing sound in the air behind you.

Two remotes rise from behind the generator. The balllike droids fly toward you, zigzagging through the air. Despite their size, their lasers pack as much punch as standard rifles.

You must destroy the remotes. They are extremely small targets so you must aim carefully. Choose to destroy both at once or one at a time.

To destroy both remotes at once: Choose your weapon. Your weapon's far-range# + your weaponry# +3 is your confront#. Roll the 12-dice so your blast will strike the first remote and ricochet to the second remote.

If your confront# is equal to or more than your roll#, add the difference +9 to your MP total. The blast strikes the first remote, then glances off at the second remote. Both remotes shatter and their remains fall to the floor. You may now proceed.

If your confront# is less than your roll#, subtract the difference from your MP total. You have missed the shot and the remotes have veered away from each other. Now you must target and destroy the remotes one at a time (below).

To destroy the remotes one at a time: Choose your weapon. Add your weaponry# to your weapon's mid-range# for your confront#. Roll the 6-dice to fire at the first remote.

If your confront# is equal to or more than your roll#, add the difference to your MP total. Repeat this confront to fire upon the second remote. After you have destroyed both remotes, you may proceed.

If your confront# is less than your roll#, subtract the difference from your MP total. Now add +1 to your confront# for your new confront#. Roll the 12-dice to shoot the first remote.

> *If your new confront# is equal to or more than your roll#*, add the difference to your MP total. Repeat this confront to shoot the second remote. After the second remote is shattered, you may proceed.
>
> *If your new confront# is less than your roll#*, subtract the difference from your MP total. Repeat this confront with your new confront# until you have destroyed both remotes, then you may proceed.

As the remotes shatter against the floor, you turn to set the timer on the bomb.

To set the timer on the bomb: Your skill# +2 is your confront#. Roll the 6-dice to activate the timing mechanism on the bomb.

> *If your confront# is equal to or more than your roll#*, add the difference to your MP total. The timer starts ticking and you may now proceed.
>
> *If your confront# is less than your roll#*, subtract the difference from your MP total. Your fingers tremble. Repeat this confront until you have set the timer, then proceed.

With the bomb ticking away, you run away from the generator, heading for the main door. You can only hope that Boonda has managed to open it.

Running through the factory, you notice that much of the manufacturing equipment has been destroyed. Burned assembly cables dangle uselessly from the ceiling, and conveyer belt rollers have been chopped into small pieces. Most of the damage appears to have been caused by some kind of laser cutting tool. As you approach the main door, a large figure suddenly steps out from the shadows and blocks the doorway.

It is a droid, a tall ASP-19 with a single green visual sensor glowing in the dim corridor. Its body appears to have been extensively modified, having longer arms and thicker joints than the typical design. From one of the ASP's manual claws, a short rod suddenly illuminates and extends. Impossible as it may seem, the ASP is carrying a lightsaber.

You have no idea how the ASP obtained such a relic, but you know that the droid is not going to just let you pass through the doorway. The bomb's timer ticks behind you.

You can choose to evade, or confuse, or combat the lightsaber-wielding ASP. If you evade, choose to do so with or without Power.

To evade the ASP droid (using Power)*: Choose your Evasion Power. Your Power's low-resist# + your stealth# + your Power# is your confront#. Roll the 6-dice to move past the ASP without drawing its attention.

> *If your confront# is equal to or more than your roll#,* add the difference +3 to your MP total. The ASP's head turns from side to side, searching for you, but you have already escaped. You may proceed.

If your confront# is less than your roll#, subtract the difference from your MP total. You have tripped and the ASP turns to attack you. You must combat the droid (below).

Note: This counts as one of two Power uses you are allowed on this Mission.

To evade the ASP droid (without Power): Add your stealth# +1 to your strength# +2 for your confront#. Roll the 12-dice and prepare to run and jump over the ASP droid.

If your confront# is equal to or more than your roll#, add the difference +3 to your MP total. Leaping high into the air, you pass over the ASP and hit the ground running. The droid is too big to follow you through the door and you may proceed.

If your confront# is less than your roll#, subtract the difference from your MP total. In your attempt to leap over the droid, you bump into the ASP's shoulder. The droid takes a quick step backward, totally blocking your exit. You must now combat it (below).

To confuse the ASP droid (using Power)*: Choose your Confusion Power. Your stealth# + your Power's mid-resist# + your Power# is your confront#. You maneuver to dizzy the droid into confusion. Roll the 6-dice.

If your confront# is equal to or more than your roll#, add the difference +4 to your MP total. The ASP's visual sensor ricochets in the wrong direction. The ASP stumbles away from the door and you may now proceed.

If your confront# is lower than your roll#, subtract the difference from your MP total. The ASP droid is not confused. You must combat it (below).

***Note:** This counts as one of two Power uses you are allowed on this Mission.

To combat the ASP droid: Choose your weapon. Add your weaponry# to your weapon's mid-range# +1 for your confront#. Take quick and careful aim at the ASP's visual sensor. Roll the 12-dice to shoot the sensor and blind the ASP.

If your confront# is equal to or more than your roll#, add the difference +4 to your MP total. The ASP's visual sensor explodes and the droid fails to find your position. The ASP stumbles away from the doorway and you may now proceed.

If your confront# is less than your roll#, subtract the difference from your MP total. Now add +2 to your confront# for your new confront#. Roll the 12-dice again to shoot the ASP in the head.

If your new confront# is equal to or more than your roll#, add the difference to your MP total. The ASP's head rocks hard to the side, sending a shower of sparks high into the air. You may now proceed.

If your new confront# is less than your roll#, subtract the difference from your MP total. The droid grabs hold of you with its lethal arms. You must break its grip (below).

To escape the ASP's grip: Your strength# +2 is your confront#. Roll the 6-dice to slip away from the ASP's grasping arms.

> *If your confront# is equal to or more than your roll#,* you pull away just in time. Now combat the ASP droid (above).
>
> *If your confront# is lower than your roll#,* subtract the difference from your MP total. You must try again. Repeat this confront until you have pulled free. Then combat the ASP droid again (above).

Racing out of the factory, you glance at your chronometer. The bomb will explode in less than ten seconds.

"Over here!" Boonda yells. The Hutt is peering over the edge of a wide sheet of plastoid that he has removed from the doorway and stuck in the ground. "Dive behind this shield!"

To dive behind the plastoid panel: Add your strength# to your stealth# for your confront#. Roll the 6-dice to leap forward, diving behind the protective plastoid panel.

> *If your confront# is equal to or more than your roll#,* add the difference +5 to your MP total. You are protected by the plastoid shield when the factory explodes.
>
> *If your confront# is lower than your roll#,* subtract 15 MP from your MP total. You miss the shield and will be hit by debris.

The factory walls tear outward as the building explodes from within. As the immediate shock wave passes over you, followed by smoke and fire, you realize you might not have survived without Boonda's help.

"You almost didn't make it out in time!" Boonda observes. "What happened inside the factory?"

"I ran into two modified remotes and an ASP-19," you answer. "From the looks of things, they were left behind to destroy the factory themselves. They were doing a good job, too. The ASP-19 was using a lightsaber."

"A lightsaber?" Boonda echoes, genuinely startled. "I do modify ASP-19s for one customer. He uses them for his own combat training, but he insists on providing the droids' weapons. How could an ASP-19 get hold of a lightsaber?"

"Admiral Groot believes the droids are manufacturing their own weapons," you recount. "Still, a lightsaber is a bit extreme. Whoever your customer is, he must be crazy to want to have lightsaber duels with droids."

"Mind your tongue, soldier," Boonda the Hutt leers. "My customer happens to be Darth Vader."

At the mere mention of the Dark Lord of the Sith, you feel your blood run cold. If there is one man in the galaxy who deserves to be feared, it is Darth Vader.

Your thoughts are interrupted by a loud crash from the burning factory. Turning to the blazing building, you see the last thing you would have expected.

The ASP-19 leaps out from flaming ruins, carrying its lightsaber in an attack position. The droid's head is gone and exposed wires extend from its neck. Even without its visual sensor, the ASP-19 boldly lurches forward in your direction, kicking up dirt with each powerful step.

"It must still be able to hear us with its audial receivers!" you exclaim as the droid approaches.

"Then stop talking!" Boonda yelps, looking for a place to hide.

You must destroy the ASP-19.

To destroy the ASP-19: Choose your weapon. Add your weaponry# to your weapon's close-range# for your confront#. Roll the 6-dice to combat the menacing droid.

If your confront# is equal to or more than your roll#, add the difference +8 to your MP total. Your blast fuses the droid's remaining circuits and you may proceed.

If your confront# is lower than your roll#, subtract the difference from your MP total. Now add +4 to your confront# for your new confront#. Roll the 12-dice to strike again at the oncoming droid.

If your confront# is equal to or more than your roll#, add the difference to your MP total. The droid's upper torso explodes and you may proceed.

If your new confront# is lower than your roll#, subtract the difference from your MP total. Repeat this confront with your new confront# until you have defeated the droid. Once you have destroyed the ASP-19, you may proceed.

You have destroyed Boonda's factory and stopped the ASP-19 in its tracks. Add 30 MP to your MP total (45 MP for Advanced Level players).

The ruined droid pitches forward on its metal legs, falling down toward you. Thick hands suddenly push you aside to safety. As the ASP-19 smashes to the ground, you suddenly realize that Boonda the Hutt may have just saved your life . . . for the second time.

"You had better check on your admiral and captain," Boonda suggests as he brushes the dirt from his hands. "I would appreciate it if you told them I made every effort to help you."

"I'll tell them," you promise. "For a Hutt, you're quite a fighter."

"You're not bad yourself," Boonda compliments you. "If you don't mind my saying so, the Empire is lucky to have a soldier like you. But if you ever want to leave your service to the Empire, I would be happy to employ you."

"Thanks," you reply, considering the Hutt's offer. "I'll think about it. But as long as those droids are still on the *Decimator*, I have a lot of work to do."

You have made a new ally in the fight against the battle droids. Reward yourself 120 MP (170 MP for Advanced Level players).

The After-Mission

Boonda the Hutt stood on a hill and watched his factory burn. The fire had spread to his fortress, and black smoke billowed from the high windows. As he watched the structures buckle and collapse, he thought of how well he had done over the years. On this remote moon, he had created a successful business. He had also done an impressive job in helping blow up his own property.

The Imperial soldier who aided Boonda against the droids had returned to Admiral Groot and Captain Pelvin. The soldier had promised to explain the situation to his commanding officers and tell them that Boonda was not to blame for the droids. The Hutt was confident the matter would be resolved.

Another tower burst into flame and a smile crossed the Hutt's broad green face. "Heck," he said to himself, "I wanted to build a new factory anyway!" Boonda could afford to be philosophical. Despite his ethical business practices, Boonda had one thing in common with his fellow Hutts: He was extremely well-insured.

A thundering noise caused Boonda to glance upward. Descending through the clouds, a *Victory*-class Star Destroyer soared down toward the burning factory. Boonda knew it had to be the *Decimator*.

The Imperial ship's repulsorlift engines kicked in and it hovered over the factory. Suddenly, a loud humming sound filled the air as the *Decimator* activated its powerful tractor beam.

The tractor beam locked onto one of the factory's outer buildings, and the structure trembled under the gravitational pull. The building was once a freight container, but Boonda had long ago transformed it into a storage warehouse, mooring it to a permanent foundation. Smoke poured from the container's upper vents.

To Boonda's amazement, the tractor beam yanked the old container away from its foundation. As the fire-filled structure rose up to the docking bay of the *Decimator*, Boonda realized the droids must have tampered with the freight container's moorings.

Boonda did not know why the droids would want the freight container. As best as he could remember, it was filled with nothing but old junk. Boonda felt uneasy as the carrier entered the *Decimator*'s docking bay.

As the Imperial ship rose away from the factory and blasted away from Boonda's Moon, the Hutt decided it might be wise to forget about the freight container entirely.

Minutes later, the Chariot LAV arrived. Captain Pelvin and Admiral Groot exited the ship and approached Boonda. Admiral Groot had a bump on his head. Captain Pelvin had a black eye.

Pointing to the Imperial soldier seated in the Chariot's cockpit, Admiral Groot declared, "Our young friend in there seems to be convinced you're innocent of any wrongdoing, Boonda."

"Your soldier is correct, Admiral," the Hutt answered. "I deeply regret what has happened today. I cannot explain the droids' actions, but I will do everything in my power to stop them."

"You can start by telling us what just happened here," Captain Pelvin stated. "Three kilometers back, we spotted the *Decimator* hovering over your factory, then we saw it blast off. Why did the droids return to the factory?"

Boonda surveyed the flaming ruins of his factory. "I have no idea why they returned, Captain," Boonda answered, telling the truth without mentioning the storage container. Just then, a loud explosion rocked the upper half of the Hutt's fortress. Watching the jets of flame spiral up into the sky, Boonda mused, "Maybe the droids just wanted to see the fireworks?"

In the *Decimator*'s docking bay, BP-A1, BP-A2, and K-2PQ lowered their fire extinguishers and watched as Forwun opened the doors of the freight container. There was still some smoke in the container, but the fire had been put out. Moving forward, the droids stared at the cargo within the container.

"Goodness!" BP-A1 remarked, hovering backward.

"Gracious!" BP-A2 added, soaring quickly behind BP-A1.

"Aw, they don't look so tough," K-2PQ muttered bravely. The cooking droid's knives rattled in his seven manual claws.

Inside the freight container, one hundred droids stood closely packed and ready for battle. They resembled modified ASP-19s, but all carried additional armor plating and bore dozens of weapons. Even in their deactivated state, each lethal droid appeared capable of extensive destruction.

"Don't worry," Forwun commented to the nervous droids. "They're on our side. I should know — I designed them myself. They will aid us in our war against all organic creatures!"

"Are you going to activate them, sir?" K-2PQ inquired.

"Not yet," Forwun replied. "These battle droids will be activated when we reach our first destination."

Adjusting his broadband antennae, Forwun signaled to the droids on the *Decimator*'s bridge. "This is Wuntoo Forcee Forwun. Set course for the planet . . . Tatooine!"

NEXT MISSION: SHOWDOWN IN MOS EISLEY!